The Camptown Races

Kevin O'Malley
American Editions • Columbus, Ohio

For Ferdinand

©1996 Kevin O'Malley
Book Design by Randy Meredith

Published in 1996 by American Editions
150 E. Wilson Bridge Road, Suite 145
Columbus, OH 43085

American Editions is an imprint of American Education Publishing.

ISBN 1-56189-399-5
Printed in the United States of America

Oh, what a day it was at the Camptown Races! The flags were flying. The bands were playing. All the fine ladies and gents were dressed in their best.

The day started with a parade around the track.
First came the jockeys dressed in their silks.

Next came the horses all groomed and ready for racing.
Last came the owners in big tall hats.

Then onto the track swaggered big Joe McRuffin, with his horse behind him. It was the biggest and strongest horse the crowd had ever seen.

McRuffin stood in front of the crowd and yelled at the top of his lungs, "If any animal racing today can beat my fine horse, I'll kiss that animal right on the lips."

A whisper went through the crowd. The winner of the race would win ten-thousand dollars and McRuffin seemed so sure his horse would win the race.

Everyone raced to the window to change their bets.

In a field, just beyond the track, there was a farmer out plowing his fields.

He had been plowing all morning and his old muley cow
was tired and needed a rest.

So he unhooked the harness and the two of them sat down
to watch the race.

The two didn't rest long! The farmer and the cow had sat down in a nest of bees.

The farmer jumped on the cow's back. The cow took off and they raced around and around the field with the bees right behind them.

Then onto the track they zoomed.

The bees were in hot pursuit.

The race had started and the crowd was cheering for McRuffin's horse.

Then they saw the cow!

The farmer and the cow were a good way back, but they were getting closer.

Soon, they were half the distance to the pack.

Next, they were in the pack.

Then they were nose to nose with McRuffin and his horse.
It was a battle through the final turn.

But the cow won the race!

The farmer was surprised to discover he had just won tenthousand dollars.

The cow was even more surprised when McRuffin kissed her right on the lips.

Now in the field just beyond the track, there is a farmer on a shiny new tractor. And there are bees with a brand new hive. And there is the old muley cow sitting in the shade munching on green grass all day long.